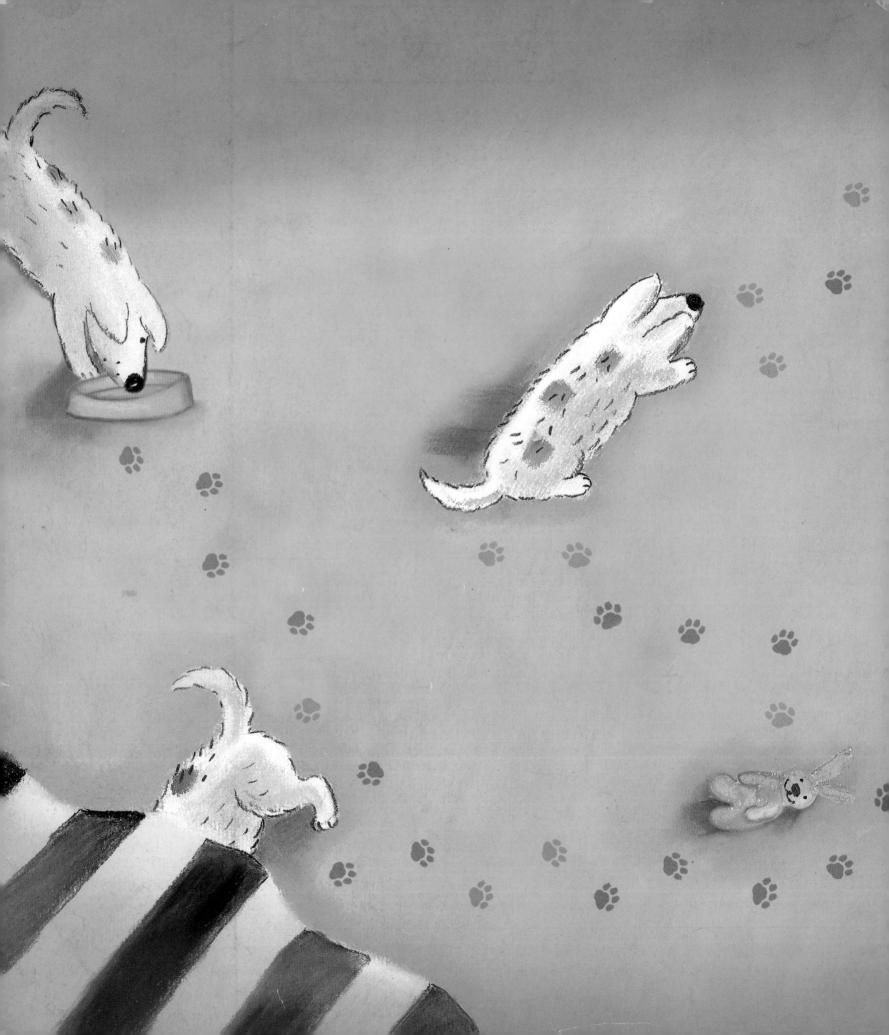

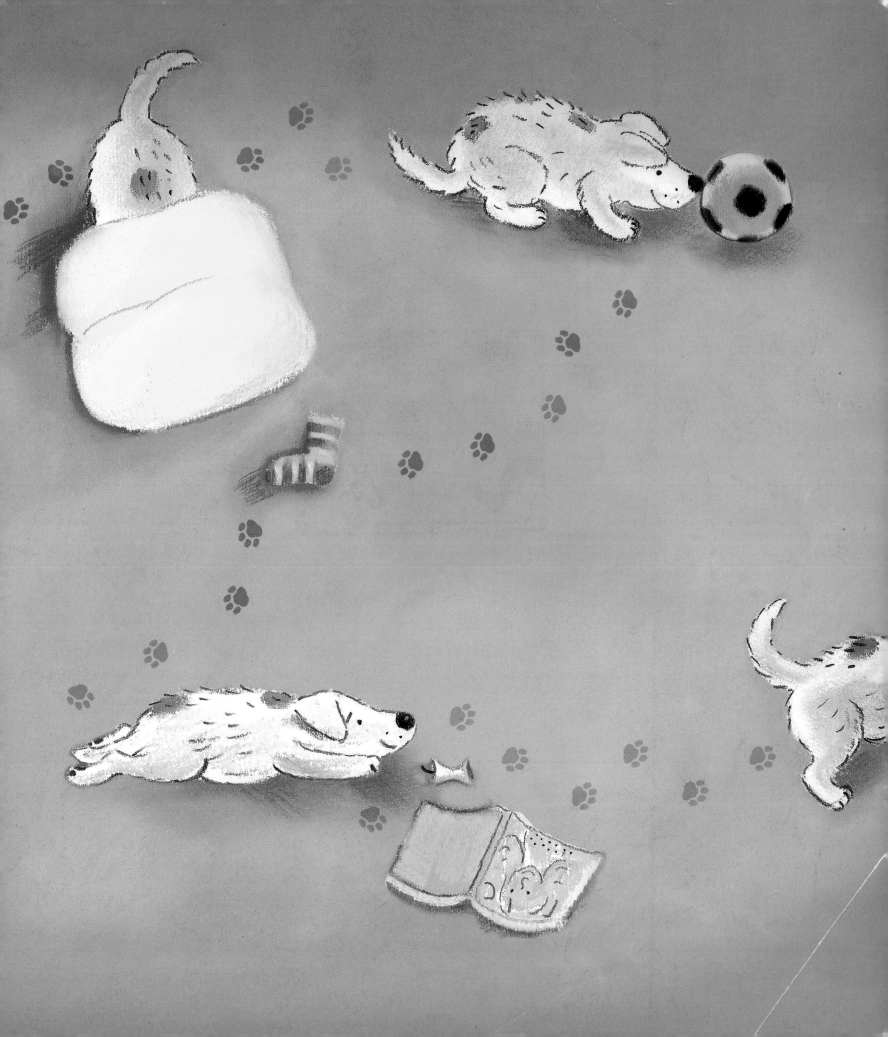

For darling Grace and her grandma ~
HO

For my sister ~
RR

First published in 2011 by Scholastic Children's Books
Euston House, 24 Eversholt Street
London NW1 1DB
a division of Scholastic Ltd
www.scholastic.co.uk
London ~ New York ~ Toronto ~ Sydney ~ Auckland
Mexico City ~ New Delhi ~ Hong Kong

Text copyright © 2011 Hiawyn Oram
Illustrations copyright © 2011 Rosie Reeve

HB ISBN 978 1407 10934 3
PB ISBN 978 1407 10935 0

My Friend Fred

Written by

Hiawyn Oram

Illustrated by

Rosie Reeve

SCHOLASTIC

This is Fred.

My friend Fred.

My sister, Clara, who has lots of friends, says:

"No, Rose, he is not yours.
He is ours. Our family dog."

I do not argue but I think, No, Clara,
you are wrong. Fred is mine.
My friend Fred.

I know he is mine because he is always there
when I open my eyes in the morning.

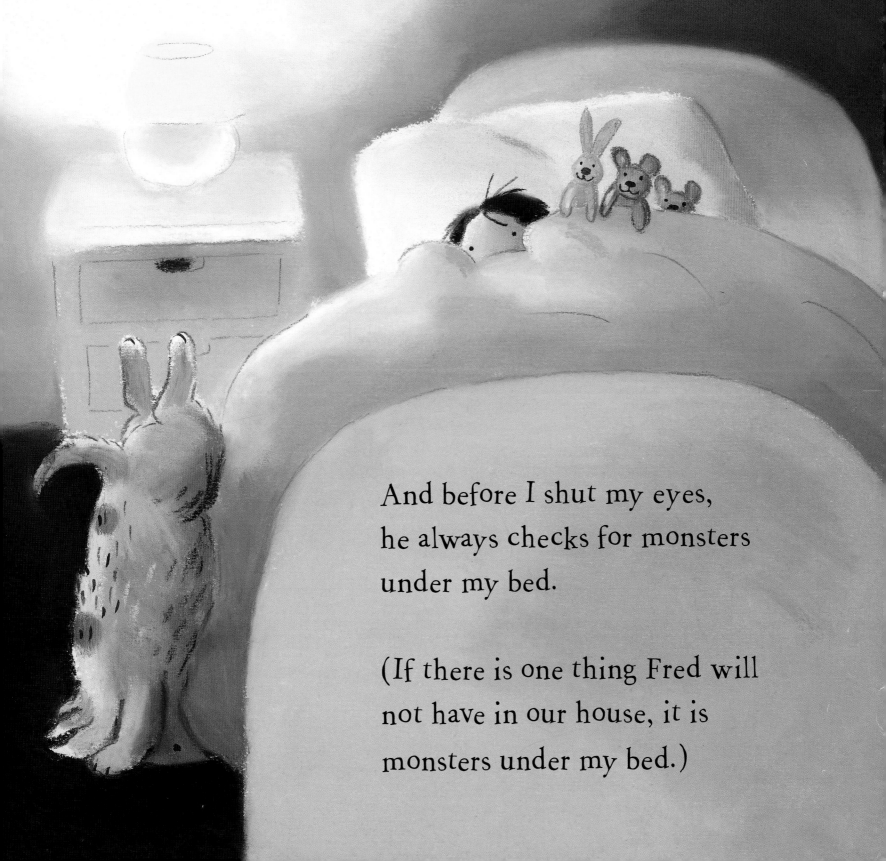

He is always there when
I shut my eyes at night.

And before I shut my eyes,
he always checks for monsters
under my bed.

(If there is one thing Fred will
not have in our house, it is
monsters under my bed.)

He likes the same stories I like.
My favourites are his favourites.
And he likes the pictures just
as much as I do.

When I am playing,
he plays with me.

When I am running
like the wind,
he runs with me.

When I am lying around on a bean bag talking to myself, he lies around too.

We lie around together.

Me and my friend Fred.

And that's not all.

When I lose things, Fred tries to find them for me.
He found Ned Bear the time Ned got himself
dropped in the pond.

He found my shoe with the plum on it
when I thought it was gone forever.

(My shoe with the plum on it is for this foot.
It goes with my shoe with the cherry on it,
which is for this foot. Together they are
my favourites.)

Sniff!

And he always seems to know where

Sniff!

to find my important bag with my name on it.

Pant, Pant!

Found it!

(This bag will be my school bag when I
go to school, which could be any day now
so it is important that I do not suddenly
find I can't remember where it is.)

Even so, even with all these reasons piled up
as high as a giant beanstalk, Clara goes on and on.

"Grow up, Rose.
Fred is ours.

Our family dog."

One day, when a lot of her friends came over,
she got a ball and said,

"Come on, Fred
the Family Dog.
Come and play
ball with us."

And that was cheating because she knows Fred cannot say no to a ball. Even if a giant who ate little dogs for lunch said, "Come on, Fred, come and play ball with me," Fred could not say no.

So I picked him up, took him to my room . . .

And shut
the door tight.

"Fred," I said, "I think there is a scary monster under my bed."

I got out our favourite books and said, "Let's look at these for hours and hours until all Clara's friends go home."

But Fred did not check for anything under the bed. And he did not want to look at books with me.

Rumpty Tumpty

A Dog is not a Cat

He pressed his nose against
the window and drooled
and scratched.

He lay by my
shut-tight door
and whimpered
and whined.

I listened from behind my books
until, in a flash, I suddenly understood
what he was trying to say.

And now I did understand,
it was easy-peasy and I
opened my shut-tight
door and we ran outside.

"All right, Clara," I said. "Friends don't keep their friends all to themselves all of the time. So here he is.

The Family Dog.
Our friend Fred."

"Thanks, Rose," barked Fred,
already leaping for the ball.
"Thanks, Rose," said Clara's friends.

"Thanks, Rose," said Clara.
"This is very big of you."

And I agree it **was** big of me,
but then I can be big when I
want to be, especially because
I know

"**ours**"

is only a **word**

and whatever anyone says,
really

that dog will

always

mostly

be . . .

my friend Fred.

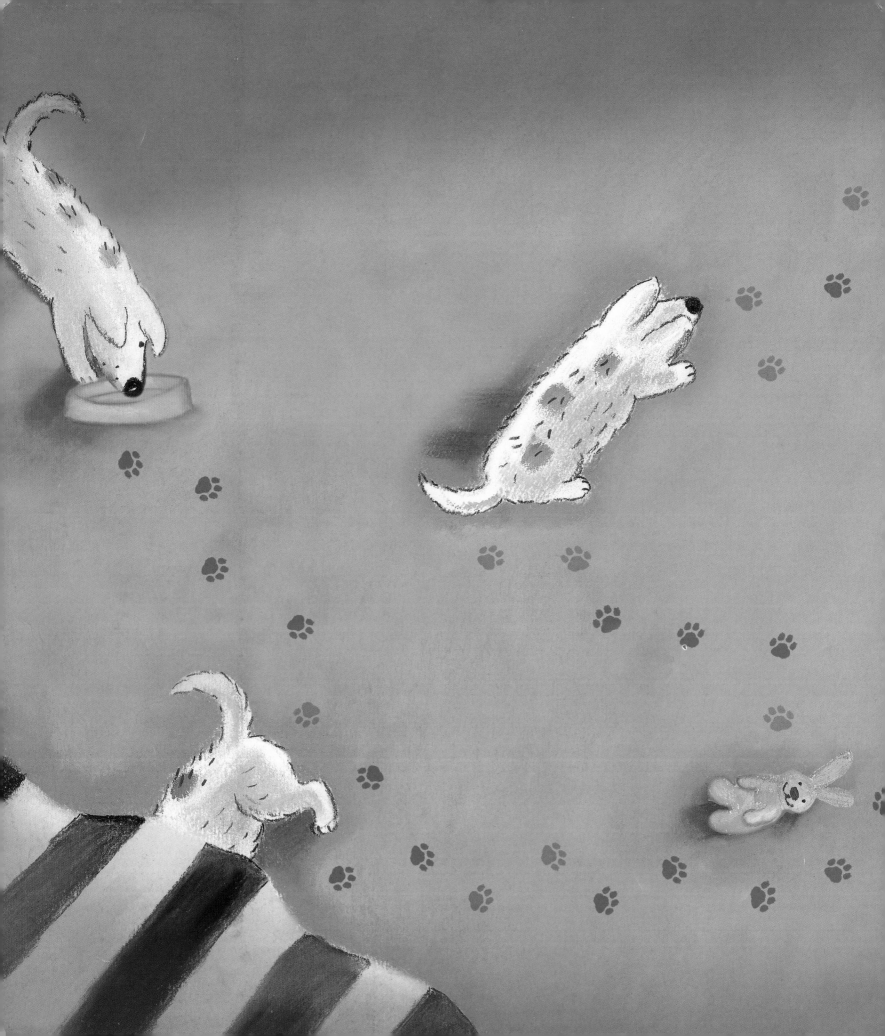